WARRIOR'S WISDOM

WARRIOR'S WISDOM

The Combat Guide
to Corporate Life

Major Arthur L. Clark,
U.S.M.C.R.

A PERIGEE BOOK

A Perigee Book
Published by The Berkley Publishing Group
200 Madison Avenue
New York, NY 10016

First edition: June 1997

Published simultaneously in Canada.

The Putnam Berkley World Wide Web site address is
http://www.berkley.com

Library of Congress Cataloging-in-Publication Data
Clark, Arthur L.
    Warrior's wisdom : the combat guide to corporate life / Major
Arthur L. Clark. — 1st ed.
        p.   cm.
    "A Perigee book."
    Includes bibliographical references.
    ISBN 0-399-51938-6
    1. Leadership—Quotations, maxims, etc. 2. Courage—Quotations,
maxims, etc. 3. Industrial management—Quotations, maxims, etc.
4. Business logistics—Quotations, maxims, etc. I. Title.
HD57.7.C537   1997
658.4'092—dc20   96-46200
                                                                         CIP

Printed in the United States of America

10   9   8   7   6   5   4   3   2   1

For my family

There is one source, O Athenians of
all your defeats. It is that your
citizens have ceased to be soldiers.
Demosthenes
383–322 B.C.

If we only act for ourselves, to
neglect the study of history is not
prudent, if we are entrusted with the
care of others, it is not just.
Samuel Johnson
1709–84

Contents

Acknowledgments   xi

Introduction   xiii

PART I: THE SOUL OF THE WARRIOR

Section 1: Becoming a Warrior   3

Section 2: The Making of a Leader   21

PART II: THE ORGANIZATION

Section 1: Chain of Command   37

Section 2: Discipline, Training, and Morale   49

PART III: PREPARING FOR BATTLE

Section 1: Administration (Human Resources)   71

Section 2: Intelligence (Know the Competition, Market Research, Concealing Your Corporate Strategy from Competitors)   75

Section 3: Operations   77

Section 4: Logistics (Supply and Maintenance)   89

PART IV: COROLLARIES AND CAUTIONS

Conclusion   103

Bibliography   105

Acknowledgments

This book would not have been possible without the kindness and assistance of many fine individuals. Julie Merberg, Hardy Justice, and Suzanne Bober of Perigee Books had both the faith and patience to see the project through. Stephanie Asbridge, Thomas Barcus, Jeffery Goodes, Jeremy Katz, Linda Lutha, Robert and Anne Rabuck, and Veronica Saffo were instrumental in helping to prepare the manuscript. Finally, thanks to my family and friends, who provided encouragement and support along the way.

Introduction

Some readers may find it unsettling that the warrior's way of life and the lessons of war should be
offered as a guide to daily living. At first glance,
war and its attendant effects—cruelty, suffering, and
death—seem to offer little to those who ponder the challenges of daily existence. Yet no other human endeavor
presents such challenges or affords so great an opportunity for man to demonstrate his best and worst qualities.

From the time they are boys, most men are intrigued by war, as evidenced by the games they play, their favorite stories, and their most beloved heroes. This inclination to things military is due less to man's inherently violent nature, as some might argue, than to a realization that the qualities that make for great commanders and armies are equally helpful when facing the challenges and struggles of daily life.

Courage, self-discipline, and sacrifice are as necessary in building relationships as they are in waging battle. Leadership and organizational skills and a willingness to take risks are essential to the team captain, the corporate executive, and the general. Therefore it seems logical that if we can learn to capture the warrior's spirit and bring to daily life the same degree of commitment that the warrior brings to battle, we might have greater chances for success on any battlefield.

Through short essays and quotations, this book highlights the positive aspects of warriors and the unique characteristics of those who lead them. Part I outlines the qualities necessary to become a warrior and a leader. Part II examines the organization of the force, while Part III focuses on the elements of battle preparation. Last, Part IV offers invaluable advice to heed when navigating the rough terrain of the battlefield. Each section may be read independently, and it is hoped that the book will appeal to both military and corporate professionals. To this end, where military terminology does not coincide with the language of the business world, corresponding corporate terms are provided. Because the quest for excellence and leadership is both enduring and universal, the quotations selected have drawn upon a wide range of military as well as political, religious, and social commentators. Their insights span centuries and cultures and reflect the age-old concern for both individual and collective achievement.

Women do not appear prominently in these pages, yet this does not imply that they do not or should not follow the way of the warrior. Throughout history women have been both able students and practitioners of war; Barbara Tuchman, Jeanne Kirkpatrick, Margaret Thatcher, Elizabeth I, and St. Joan of Arc are but a few of the more prominent examples. Over the course of time, however, war has been primarily a male endeavor. For this reason men's thoughts command this work and the masculine tense is used throughout the book. The way of the warrior is not an easy vocation, but is open to all men and women who are willing to bring a commitment to excellence and service to every aspect of their lives.

This book is a study of attitude rather than tactics and technology. The warrior spirit concerns itself with what the nineteenth-century military strategist Carl von Clausewitz called the moral factors—those elements that do not lend themselves to easy quantification on a spreadsheet, but nonetheless have great importance. More simply, the warrior spirit is about character. Unlike technology or theories of management, character is enduring. When we cultivate a sense of character within ourselves and nurture it in others, we honor the warrior by living a life of integrity and accomplishment.

WARRIOR'S WISDOM

PART I

THE SOUL
OF THE
WARRIOR

Becoming
a Warrior

Within the modern military there are thousands of military occupations—infantry, pilot, mechanic, medic, etc.—but the most successful units are those who have defined themselves not by skills but by the fact that they're first and foremost soldiers, sailors, airmen, or Marines. Likewise successful soldiers on the corporate battlefield are not simply practitioners of a skill, but dedicated warriors.

The qualities that define the warrior are these:

The warrior is courageous.
The warrior is self-disciplined.
The warrior is physically fit.
The warrior is resolute.
The warrior has faith.

It is important to note that these qualities are not merely isolated characteristics. Rather, each is mutually reinforcing. Faith often requires physical and moral courage. If not steeled with both self-discipline and physical toughness, even the most resolute soldier will falter. The warrior strives to develop each of these attributes, knowing that progress in one area leads to benefits in another.

The Warrior Is Courageous

Courage is the best gift of all: courage stands before everything. It is what preserves our liberty, safety, life, our homes and parents, our country and children. Courage comprises all things; a man with courage has every blessing.

Platus, <u>Amphitro</u>. Third century B.C.

Fortune favors the Brave.

Terence, <u>Phormio</u>, c. 160 B.C.

In his seminal work, *On War*, the Prussian general and famed military strategist Carl von Clausewitz identified two kinds of bravery: courage in the face of physical danger and the ability to accept responsibility for one's actions "either before the tribunal of some outside power or before the court of one's own conscience." While he focused on the former in his writings, he did not discount the importance of the latter. Indeed, the morally courageous man is often able to overcome material shortcomings if confronted by a foe who lacks this quality. Both physical and moral courage remain essential to the warrior and the businessman of today.

PHYSICAL COURAGE

It is no mere coincidence that in reviewing the lives of successful leaders in the contemporary business world, physical courage is a common theme and a prized attribute. Many began to develop this trait as boys—in the arena of sports—and continue to pursue it throughout life. Ted Turner's race for America's Cup, Ross Perot's taste for speedboat competition, and the annual boxing matches between the traders in the Chicago futures market all illustrate this notion perfectly. These individuals understand that success is a by-product of self-confidence, and this confidence can only be developed and maintained in the realm of physical danger. In doing so, they continue the martial tradition of warriors throughout time and give themselves an edge over softer opponents.

Physical courage is developed through a vigorous program of conditioning and exercise, during which the warrior is trained to control his fear while accomplishing his mission. If you look beyond the suits of most successful corporate executives you will find a competitive nature with a taste for danger acquired either in sports or military service. More important, when you look at the record of great armies or companies that have been defeated, you will find that early strength and ardor have given way to concerns for comfort and complacency, leaving them unable to deal with a hardened and resourceful opponent on an ever changing battlefield.

> Courage conquers all things, it even gives strength to the body.
>
> Ovid, Ex Ponto, A.D.13

> Valor is the contempt of death and pain.
>
> Tacitus, A.D.55–117

> No Courage is so bold as that forced by utter desperation.
>
> Seneca, De Clemetia, A.D. 55

> That's courage—to take hard knocks like a man when occasions call.
>
> Platus, Asinerra, Third century B.C.

> It is better to live one day as a lion than a hundred years as a sheep.
>
> Italian proverb

> Be strong, and quit yourselves like men.
>
> Samuel 4:9

> Tis true that we are in great danger;
> The greater therefore should our courage be.
>
> Shakespeare, Henry V, IV, I

> The battle is not to the strong alone; it is to the vigilant, the active, the brave.
>
> Patrick Henry to the Virginia Convention, 23 March 1775

A man of courage never wants of weapons.

Thomas Fuller, <u>Gnomologia</u> #302, 1608–91

All men are frightened. The more intelligent they are, the more they are frightened. The courageous man is the man who forces himself, in spite of his fear, to carry on. Discipline, pride, self-respect, self-confidence, and love of glory are attributes which will make a man courageous even when he is afraid.

George S. Patton, <u>War As I Knew It</u>, 1947

MORAL COURAGE

Before a soldier enters the ranks of the army, he should already recognize the value of moral courage, the ability to act correctly when faced with a choice between right and wrong. Sadly, it is becoming all too common to find that the fundamental principles of moral bravery have not been taught or are only honored in the breech. The warrior lives by a code of conduct that governs his dealings with others. Temptations big and small are present on every battlefield. The warrior who compromises himself out of ambition, greed, or fear not only places himself at risk, but also undermines the trust necessary for his organization to function successfully.

Oh friends be men and let your hearts be strong.
And let no warrior in the heat of fight
Do what may bring him shame in others' eyes.

For more of those who shrink from shame are safe
than fall in battle, while with those who
flee is neither glory nor reprieve from death.
Homer, The Iliad,V, 800 B.C.

To see what is right and not to do it is want of courage.
Confucius, 551–479 B.C.

Courage is that virtue which champions the cause of right.
Cicero, De Officiis, 45 B.C.

Who is the invincible man? He whom nothing which is
outside the sphere of his moral purpose can dismay.
Epictetus, Discourses, A.D. 100

Cowards die many times before their death;
The valiant never taste death but once.
Shakespeare, Julius Caesar, II, 2

True courage is to do without witness everything that one
is capable of doing before all the world.
La Rochefoucauld, Maxims, #216, 1665

I would define true courage to be a perfect sensibility of
the measure of danger and a mental willingness to incur
it.
William T. Sherman, Personal Memoirs, 1875

The Warrior Is
Self-Disciplined

Self-control is the chief element in self-respect, and self-respect is the chief element in courage.

Thucydides, <u>The History of the Peloponnesian Wars</u>, 404 B.C.

Self-discipline implies the ability to resist temptation and impose limits and set goals for personal achievement. This is the private battle the warrior wages each day. The outcome of this personal struggle often determines success or failure on life's more public battlefields. The warrior is on time. His personal appearance and demeanor mark him as a professional. He starts each day with a clear plan of action. He takes pride in his work and delivers on the promises he makes. Furthermore, like Apache braves of old, he can forgo instant gratification for the sake of duty or in order to achieve goals that require time and careful, deliberate planning.

Learn to obey before you command.

Solon of Athens, 638–559 B.C.

He is strong who conquers others, but he who conquers himself is mighty.

Lao Tze, <u>The Way of Virtue</u>, 550 B.C.

It is discipline that makes one feel safe, while the lack of discipline has destroyed many people before now.

Xenophon, Speech at the Battle of Cunaxa, 401 B.C.

The victory over self is of all victories the first and the best.

Plato, Laws, 340 B.C.

I count him braver who overcomes his desires than him who conquers his enemies, the hardest victory is victory over self.

Aristotle, Apothegm, 340 B.C.

Subdue your angry spirit, you will subdue all else.

Ovid, Herodes, 10 B.C.

Self-discipline is that which, next to virtue, truly and essentially raises one man above another.

Joseph Addison, 1672–1719

I cannot trust a man to control others who cannot control himself.

Robert E. Lee, 1807–70

True military discipline stems not from knowledge but habit.

Gen. Hans Von Seeckt, 1866–1936

The Warrior Is
Physically Fit

What can a soldier do who charges when out of breath?
Vegetius, <u>De Re Militari</u>, 378 B.C.

Physical hardship is part and parcel of the combat experience. The most successful warriors are those who have developed physical and mental stamina before heading into battle. On an individual basis, a fit warrior can better handle the stress and fatigue of daily battle and projects an air of confidence and self-discipline. Taken as a whole, an army of warriors who are fit *creates* a noticeably more positive *impression* than troops who look like they might not live through, let alone survive, the next engagement. Additionally, a fit army not only is more productive but also has lower rates of injury and health-care expenses. Whether military or corporate, combat often requires the long march. History remembers Hannibal or the Marines who marched out of the Chosin Reservoir because they possessed the physical toughness to achieve greatness.

By constant exercise one develops freedom of movement—for virtuous deeds.
Diogenes, Third century A.D.

Effeminacy was the chief cause of the ruin of the Roman legions. Those formidable soldiers, who had borne the helmet buckler and breastplate in times of the Scipios under the burning sun of Africa, found them too heavy in the cool climates of Germany and Gaul, and then the empire was lost.

Jomini, Précis sur l'art de la Guerre, 1838

Nations have passed away and left no traces. And history gives the naked cause of it—One single, simple reason, in all cases; They fell because they were not fit.

Rudyard Kipling, Tales for Scouts and Guides, 1923

I wish to preach not the doctrine of ignoble ease, but the doctrine of the strenuous life.

Theodore Roosevelt, 1858–1919

A pint of sweat will save a gallon of blood!

George S. Patton, War As I Knew It, 1947

The Warrior Is Resolute

He conquers who endures.

Persius, A.D. 34–62

Resolution, whether to endure battle or the hardships of building a successful company, is often the determining characteristic of the great warrior. Soldiers expect to endure hardship in the pursuit of victory. Sleepless nights and the risks to personal or financial security are part of the combat experience. The resolute warrior is not discouraged by momentary failure; he is not easily swayed by popular opinion which may counsel lesser goals or compromises on matters of principle. He knows that in a contest of wills both sides are pushed to the breaking point. A resolute attitude allows him to persevere against all odds.

Endure and persevere; this pain will turn to your good by and by.

Ovid, Amores, 13 B.C.

Persevere: it is thy part. Perhaps on the unhappy, happier days shall wait.

Virgil, Aneid, 19 B.C.

There is nothing which persevering effort and unceasing and diligent care cannot overcome.

Seneca, Epistulae ad Lucilium, First century A.D.

A just man falleth seven times and riseth up again.
Proverbs 24:16

God is with those who persevere.
Mohammed, The Koran, Chap. 8

If I go on, I shall die, if I stay behind I shall be dishonored. It is better to go on.
Ashanti "War Song"

A stout heart breaks bad luck.
Spanish proverb

We fight, get beat, rise, and fight again.
Nathaniel Greene, June 1781

If our numbers are small, our hearts are great.
Sir Henry Morgan before attacking Portobelo, 1667

Great extremities require extraordinary resolution. The more obstinate the resistance of an army, the greater the chances of success. How many seeming impossibilities have been accomplished by men whose only resolve was death!
Napoleon I, Maxims, 1831

If a general and his men fear death and are apprehensive over possible defeat, then they will unavoidably suffer defeat and death. But if they make up their minds from the general down to the last foot soldier, not to think of living but of standing in one place and facing death together, then, though they may have no other thought than meeting death, they will instead hold on to life and gain victory.

Yoshida Shoin, 1830–59

Tell him to go to hell.

General Zachary Taylor to Santa Anna, who demanded his surrender at Buena Vista, Mexico, 1847

Tenacity of purpose and untiring energy in the execution can repair a first mistake and baffle deeply laid plans.

Alfred Thayer Mahan, 1840–1914

Victory will come to the side which outlasts the other.

Ferdinand Foch, Battle of the Marne, 7 September 1914

We shall not flag or fail. We shall go on to the end, we shall fight in France, we shall fight in the seas and oceans, we shall fight with growing confidence and growing strength in the air, we shall defend our island, whatever the cost may be, we shall fight on the beaches, we shall fight on the landing grounds, we shall fight in the fields and in the streets, we shall fight in the hills, we shall never surrender.

Winston Churchill to Parliament after Dunkirk, 4 June 1940

Success is the result of perfection, hard work, learning from failure, loyalty to those for whom you work, and persistence.

Colin Powell, 1995

The Warrior Has Faith

A good cause makes a stout heart and a strong arm.
Thomas Fuller, <u>Gnomologia</u> #140, 1654–1734

The soldier's heart, the soldier's spirit, the soldier's soul are everything. Unless the soldier's soul sustains him, he cannot be relied on and will fail himself and his country in the end.
Gen. George C. Marshall, 1880–1959

The hardships and sacrifices of battle are often so great and prolonged that mere material reward does not compensate for its demands. A man whose services are motivated solely by money is a mercenary and not a warrior. A mercenary's loyalty is changeable and driven solely by self-interest. Since the focus of his interest is so narrow, his chance for enduring, meaningful success is slim.

A warrior has faith and because he has faith he can inspire it in others. The warrior has faith in himself and the cause for which he fights. And ultimately, he has faith in God, which provides the moral underpinning for all his actions.

FAITH IN THE CAUSE

A warrior is called to the battlefield in the service of his country, to protect the ideals he cherishes and ensure that the benefits of war will accrue to his family. On the corporate battlefield, successful companies are easy to distinguish from mere competitors by the commitment of their warriors to their products or services. These corporate warriors truly believe that they are the best at what they do and strive to protect the company's continued success. In military terms, this sense of corporate patriotism is the warrior's unflagging faith in the cause for which he fights.

> His sword the brave man draws,
> And asks no omen but his country's cause.
> Homer, The Iliad, 800 B.C.

> This empire has been acquired by men who knew their duty and had the courage to do it, who in the hour of conflict had the fear of dishonor always present to them. . . .
> Pericles, Funeral oration, The Peloponnesian War, 431 B.C.

> With God's blessing let us make thorough work of it.
> Stonewall Jackson, Beginning of the Valley Campaign, 1862

FAITH IN GOD

History is filled with numerous examples of men who have sought the assistance of God at the moment of crisis. A solid trust in God is as important today as it has been throughout the centuries. Religious belief provides the soldier with a sense of self-worth, inspires courage, reduces his sense of isolation, and restrains his baser impulses, which otherwise distract him in the heat of battle.

O God of battles, steel my soldiers hearts. Possess them not with fear, take from them now, the sense of reckoning, if the opposed numbers pluck their heart from them.

Shakespeare, Henry V, IV, I

O Lord! Thou knowest how busy I must be this day; If I forget Thee, do not Thou forget me. March on, boys!

Sir Jacob Astley, Before the Battle of Edgehill, 1642

Oh God, let me not be disgraced in my old days. Or if Thou will not help me, do not help these scoundrels, but leave us to try it ourselves.

Leopold I of Anhalt-Dessay, 14 December 1745

There are no atheists in foxholes.

Chaplain W. T. Cummings, Sermon on Bataan, March 1942

Section 2

The Making
of a Leader

An army of deer led by a lion is more to be feared than an
army of lions led by a deer.

Chabrias, 410–375 B.C.

The task of leadership is not to put greatness into hu-
manity, but to elicit it, for the greatness is already there.

John Buchan, 1875–1940

I t should be the desire of every warrior to lead others.
Leadership is the guiding force that directs the actions of individual warriors to achieve a common
goal. A leader should possess the qualities of the successful warrior but also must learn to command and inspire

others. To become a leader, one must seek to master the attributes of leadership. They are as follows:

> The leader sets the example.
> The leader is bold.
> The leader is confident.
> The leader studies his profession.
> The leader is courteous and compassionate.

The Leader Sets the Example

Everyone is bound to bear patiently the results of his own example.

Phaedrus, <u>Fables</u>, Book One, Fable 26, First century A.D.

The leader has two responsibilities: creating clear guidelines for conduct and, more important, living up to the principles he has set down. When the leader fails to provide clear guidance for warriors to follow, he finds himself at the helm of a mob, not an army. While capable of destruction, mobs seldom achieve positive or enduring results. Furthermore, mobs are quickly defeated when confronted by a disciplined and well-led opponent.

Having once set down his rules of conduct, the leader also must recognize that he is always being watched by his subordinates. His appearance, work habits, and his dealings with others are always being measured against the policies he has enforced. Nothing so quickly undermines a warrior's respect or a leader's authority as hypocrisy.

Whose life lightens, his words thunder.

Latin proverb

The people are fashioned by the example of their king.

Claudian, A.D. 340

The wise man before he speaks will consider well what he speaks, to whom he speaks, and where and when.

St. Ambrose, <u>De Officiis</u>, A.D. 340–397

He preaches well that lives well.

Cervantes, <u>Don Quixote</u>, 1604

As I would deserve and keep the kindness of this army, I must let them see that when I expose them, I would not exempt myself.

Duke of Marlborough, 1650–1772

Nothing is so contagious as example.

La Rochefoucauld, <u>Maxims</u>, 1665

I have deemed it more honorable and more profitable, to set a good example than to follow a bad one.

Thomas Jefferson, <u>Writings</u>, 1800

Men are more easily led than driven: example is better than precept.

Lord Averbury, <u>Use of Life</u>, 1894

In moments of panic, fatigue or disorganization, or when something out of the ordinary has to be demanded from [his troops], the personal example of the commander works wonders, especially if he has had the wit to create some sort of legend round himself.

Erwin Rommel, <u>The Rommel Papers</u>, 1953

Be an example to your men both in your duty and in private life. Never spare yourself, and let the troops see that you don't, in your endurance of fatigue and privation. Always be tactful and well mannered and teach your subordinates to be the same. Avoid excessive sharpness or harshness of voice, which usually indicates the man who has shortcomings of his own to hide.

Erwin Rommel, Remarks to cadets, 1938

The Leader Is Bold

The desire for safety stands against every great and noble enterprise.

Tacitus, <u>Annals</u>, c. A.D. 110

A leader is expected to solve problems, seize opportunities or create them where none exist. To accomplish this, he must be bold. When General Douglas MacArthur planned his surprise landing on Inchon against the counsel of all his advisers, when Bill McGowan of MCI took on AT&T with only three thousand dollars and an idea, they demonstrated boldness. They were not blind to the risks their operations entailed. But, they realized that to achieve success they needed to dramatically alter the battlefield or marketplace by taking risks, sometimes enormous ones. The bold man doesn't ask for guarantees or safety. He is not content with the "We have always done it that way" or "It can't be done" response. He is able to weigh relevant factors, but when it is time to act, he moves fearlessly.

A bold man is better in all things.

Homer, <u>The Odyssey</u>, 850 B.C.

The only hope of safety was in boldness.

Tacitus, <u>Histories</u>, c. A.D. 115

Boldness in business, first, second and third thing.

Thomas Fuller, <u>Gnomologia</u> #1006, 1608-1691

By boldness great fears are concealed.

Horace, Epistle, 65–8 B.C.

The gods look with favor on superior daring.

Civilius to his legions, Histories by Tacitus, c. A.D. 115

It is true I must run great risk; no gallant action was ever accomplished without danger.

John Paul Jones, 1778

First reckon, then risk.

Helmuth von Moltke, 1800–1891

Never forget that no military leader has ever become great without audacity.

Clausewitz, Principles of War, 1812

Far better to dare mighty things, to win glorious triumphs, even though checkered with defeats, than to count yourself among those poor souls, who neither enjoy much or suffer much because they live in the grey twilight which knows not victory or defeat.

Theodore Roosevelt, 1858–1919

Bold decisions give the best promise of success.

Erwin Rommel, Rules of Desert Warfare, 1891–1944

I only have to do so much compromising. There comes a time when I can say, "Do it!"

Colin Powell, 1995

The Leader Is Confident

In confidence and quietness shall be your strength.
Isaiah 30:15

Fields are won by those who believe in winning.
Thomas Higginson, 1823–1911

Confidence distinguishes leaders from followers; it is the by-product of experience, conviction, and a sense of optimism. The confident leader communicates both the possibility of success and the likelihood that it will be achieved. Whether introducing a new product, launching a company, or speaking to men on the eve of battle, a leader must create a sense of hopefulness and convince others that he has a solution to a problem and that his words are worthy of their full attention.

People sense confidence in the warrior's appearance, the tone of his voice, whether he looks them straight in the eye when he speaks to them and answers their question directly. When Henry the Fifth found himself surrounded and outnumbered on the fields of Agincourt, he didn't appear before his men and mumble, "Well, this is it, we are all going to be slaughtered." While he couldn't offer any guarantees for survival, let alone victory, he could and did provide hope. He offered a promise that their efforts would be memorable and rewarded. Because he displayed confidence in a moment of crisis, his soldiers could draw upon his reserves and commit themselves to the job ahead. The memory of the overwhelming victory by the English on that day still endures centuries later and demonstrates the power of confident leadership.

> Confidence is that feeling by which the mind embarks on great and honorable courses with a sure hope and trust in itself.
>
> Cicero, De Invention Rhetorica, 106–43 B.C.

> Lack of confidence is not the result of difficulty; the difficulty comes from lack of confidence.
>
> Seneca, Epistulae ad Lucilium, 4 B.C.–A.D. 65

> Self-confidence is the first requisite to great undertakings.
>
> Samuel Johnson, Works, 1709–84

> The most vital quality a soldier can possess is self-confidence, utter, complete, and bumptious.
>
> George S. Patton, Letter to his son at West Point, 6 June 1944

> Perpetual optimism is a force multiplier.
>
> Colin Powell, "Rules," My American Journey, 1995

The Leader Studies
His Profession

The warrior who cultivates his mind polishes his arms.
Chevalier de Boufflers, 1738–1815

Whether military or corporate, the modern battlefield is an increasingly complicated place. Leaders
are expected to be flawless managers as well as masters of
the latest technology and technique of their profession.
History is full of examples of leaders who anticipated the
impact of new technology on the battlefield, as well as
examples of those who did not, with grave human or financial consequences. General Billy Mitchell, for in-
stance, predicted the role air power would play in future
wars, while many of his contemporaries advocated—
with tragic results—trench warfare on the Western Front
during World War I. In the corporate arena, Bill Gates
was able to envision an enormous demand for personal
computers and software when his less visionary competitor, IBM, declared there was no future in that field.

A leader must master the art of macromanagement;
that is, he need not know how to build every component,
but he does need to know how to use all components effectively. He also must write well, speak persuasively, and
tend to administrative details. Commanders who are
only concerned with the big picture often learn that

these minor details are what make for an effective fighting force.

> A wise man is strong; yea, a man of knowledge increaseth
> his strength.
> Proverbs 24:5

> War is a matter of vital importance to the state, the
> province of life or death; the road to survival or ruin. It is
> mandatory that it be thoroughly studied.
> Sun Tzu, The Art of War, 400–320 B.C.

> The courage of a soldier is heightened by his knowledge
> of his profession.
> Vegetius, De Re Militari, 378 B.C.

> Knowledge is power.
> Francis Bacon, De Hereibus, 1561–1626

> War is not an affair of chance. A great deal of knowledge,
> study and meditation is necessary to conduct it well.
> Frederick the Great, Instructions to His Generals, 1747

The Leader Is Courteous and Compassionate

> The age of chivalry is gone and that of sophisters, economists and calculators has succeeded.
>
> Edmund Burke, <u>Reflections on the Revolution in France</u>, 1790

All great commanders have rightly understood that courtesy and compassion have their place in war, in dealing with an opponent as well as their own troops. Underlying any dispute involving discrimination, sexual harassment, worker's compensation, and negligence is a charge that a leader has treated his warriors in a manner unbefitting leadership. A real leader treats his warriors as his most dynamic and precious assets. He is genuinely concerned with their welfare and knows that his ability to accomplish his mission is tied to their individual and collective success. This does not mean he cannot give orders or enforce unpopular decisions, but it does mean that he must be aware of the effects of his actions on the lives of others.

> I shall maintain and defend
> the honest adoes and quarrels of all ladies of honor, widows, orphans and maids of good fame.
>
> Oath of Knighthood, Sir William Drummond, 1619

Dear Madame:

I have been shown in the files of the War Department a statement of the Adjutant General of Massachusetts that you are the mother of five sons who have died gloriously on the field of battle. I feel how weak and fruitless must be any words of mine which should attempt to beguile you from the grief of a loss so overwhelming. But I cannot refrain from tendering you the consolation that may be found in the thanks of the Republic they died to save. I pray that our heavenly Father may assuage the anguish of your bereavement, and leave you only the cherished memory of the loved and lost, and the solemn pride that must be yours to have laid so costly a sacrifice upon the altar of freedom.

Abraham Lincoln, Letter to Mrs. Lydia Bixby, 21 November 1864

But after all when you have to kill a man it costs nothing to be polite.

Winston Churchill, The Grand Alliance, 1950

Remain calm. Be kind.

Colin Powell, "Rules," My American Journey, 1995

PART II

THE

ORGANIZATION

The mass needs, and we give it leaders . . . We add good arms. We add suitable methods of fighting . . . We also add rational decentralization . . . We animate with passion . . . An iron discipline . . . secures the greatest unit . . . But it depends also on supervision, the mutual supervision of groups of men who know each other well. A wise organization of comrades in peace who shall be comrades in war . . . and now confidence appears . . . then we have an army.

Ardant du Picq, Battle Studies, 1868

The leader applies his skills and, thereby, achieves either success or failure within the structure of an organization. To develop a winning team, the leader must possess a clear understanding of the responsibilities and capabilities of every level of his unit and strive to create a winning attitude. He does this through operating within an effective chain of command, enforcing discipline within the ranks, and maintaining high morale. We will examine each of these factors in the pages that follow.

Section 1

Chain of Command

Generally, management of the many is the same as management of the few. It is a matter of organization.

Sun Tzu, <u>The Art of War</u>, 400–320 B.C.

A hierarchy must be established within any organization. A strong chain of command is needed if the efforts of the group are to be effectively directed. This section will examine the qualities appropriate to each level of the organization's chain of command—its officers and men.

Two points should be addressed, however, before evaluating the organizational chart and rank. First, the chain of command is a tool used for accomplishing the mission and should not be confused with the mission it-self. Good ideas can originate at any level of the organizational chart; the wise commander ensures that all ideas are heard and if sound, implemented. As for rank and whatever privileges it may entail, it should first and foremost be a measure of a man's responsibilities and not his ego. A lofty position does not absolve him from performing menial tasks or rolling up his sleeves when necessity demands. This is as true for the military commander as the corporate executive.

The best commanders understand the value of mingling with the troops in the field. The late Ray Kroc, the founder of McDonalds, and Sam Walton, the founder of Wal-Mart, were great advocates of this leadership style. Herb Kelleher, President of Southwest Airlines, regularly heads to the loading docks, handles baggage, and even evaluates the rest rooms on the planes. He recognizes the importance of seeing his operations in person and working alongside the individuals within his organization.

> I was informed that all the causes for delay had been reported through the "usual channels" but thus far as to those on the spot were aware nothing very much seems to have happened. It would seem better therefore to start from the other end of the "usual channels" and sound backwards to find where the delay in dealing with the matter has occurred.
>
> Winston Churchill to General Ismay, 1941

Officers

You are generals, you are officers and captains. In peacetime you got more pay and more respect than they did. Now in time of war, you ought to hold yourselves to be braver than the general mass of men.

Xenophon, 401 B.C.

Our army would be invincible if it could be properly organized and officered. There never were such men in an army before. They will go anywhere and do anything if properly led. But there is the difficulty—proper commanders.

Robert E. Lee to Stonewall Jackson, 1862

The officer ranks form the nucleus around which a successful army is built. They direct and supervise the whole force. While particular responsibilities within these ranks will vary, each member of the officer corps must maintain a high level of personal integrity and demonstrate a genuine concern for the lives of every man entrusted to his care. The decisions leaders make have a direct impact on the mission. If personal gain or ambition is the officer's sole motivation, the mission and those entrusted to his care will suffer. Also, it is important to remember that while authority, responsibility, and expectations increase from the junior officer ranks to those of general, there is no guarantee that personal capabilities will increase accordingly. Most great generals have been great captains, but not all great captains have made great generals. The qualities needed to achieve success at each level of command are different.

THE GENERAL
(President, Chief Operating Officer, Chairman of the Board)

Now there are five matters to which a general must pay strict heed. The first of these is administration; the second, preparedness; the third, determination; the fourth, prudence; and the fifth, economy. Administration means to control many as he controls few. Preparedness means that when he marches forth from the gates, he acts as if he perceives the enemy. Resolution means that when he approaches the enemy, he does not worry about life. Prudence means that although he has conquered, he acts as if he were just beginning to fight. Economy means being sparing.

Wu Ch'l, Art of War, 430–380 B.C.

As the forces in one individual after another become prostrated and can no longer be excited and supported by an effort of his own will, the whole inertia of the mass gradually rests its weight on the will of the commander. By the spark in his breast, by the light of his spirit, the spark of purpose, the light of hope must be kindled afresh in others.

Clausewitz, On War, 1832

A Commander should have profound understanding of human nature, the knack of smoothing out troubles, the power of winning affection while communicating energy and the capacity for ruthless determination where required by circumstance. He needs to generate an electrifying current and keep a cool head in applying it.

Liddell Hart, Thoughts on War, 1944

CHIEF OF STAFF
(Executive Vice Presidents, Division Heads, Deputies)

The leading qualifications which should distinguish an officer for the head of the staff are, to know the country thoroughly; to be able to conduct a reconnaissance with skill; to superintend the transmission of orders promptly; to lay down the most complicated movements intelligibly, but in a few words and with simplicity.

Napoleon I, Maxims, 1831

JUNIOR OFFICERS
(Middle and Entry-Level Management)

He is to be vigilant, temperate, active and readier to execute the orders he receives than to discuss them; strict in exercising and keeping up proper discipline among his soldiers, in obliging them to appear clean and well-dressed and to have their arms consistently polished and bright.

Vegetius, De Re Militari, 378 B.C.

He was fond of adventure, ready to lead an attack on the enemy by day or night, and when he was in an awkward position he kept his head.

Xenophon, <u>Anabasis</u>, 390 B.C.

The union of wise theory with great character will constitute a great captain.

Jomini, <u>Précis sur l'art de la Guerre</u>, 1838

While the scope of responsibilities and authority will vary by rank, there are three general principles that apply to officers at all levels: know yourself, know your business, know your men.

KNOW YOURSELF

First find the man in yourself, if you seek to inspire manliness in others.

Bronson Alcott, 1799–1888

As an officer begins a new assignment after learning what is expected of him for the mission at hand, he needs to assess his strengths and weaknesses. Likewise, he must find men in his organization who can assist in his areas of weakness. If the task involves a certain expertise that he does not currently possess, he finds the expert and has him bring him up to speed. The officer must consistently weigh the critical element of his mission against his own strengths and weaknesses and use this method of assessment in achieving his overall goals.

KNOW YOUR BUSINESS

The ordinary soldier has a surprisingly good nose for what is true and what is false.

Erwin Rommel, The Rommel Papers, 1953

You can't snow the troops.

U.S. Marine Corps saying

An officer is expected to possess a basic level of knowledge about the organization as a whole and his specific responsibilities. If he is to master his profession, meet his obligations, and stay current with developments, continuous study is a necessity. His junior ranks will notice his lack of competence more quickly than his peers and superiors, and rank alone will not make up for shortcomings. On occasion, he may be thrust into a position for which he may not be prepared. If so, he should acknowledge his ignorance and work with his subordinates to become an expert. They will be far more willing to go out of their way to help him if he demonstrates a desire to learn. And his superiors will have greater respect for a man who is driven to try than for one who is ignorant and chooses to remain so.

KNOW YOUR MEN

The relation between officers and men should in no sense be that of superior and inferior, nor that of master and servant, but rather that of teacher and scholar. In fact, it should partake of the nature of the relation between father and son, to the extent that officers, especially commanding officers, are responsible for the physical, mental and morale welfare, as well as discipline and military training of young men under their command.

Gen. John A. Lejeune, USMC, Marine Corps Manual, 1920

The officer's men are his most precious resource; to lead them he must know them. Enlisted men do not expect officers to be their friends or drinking buddies. They do expect their assistance in getting the job done, concern for their professional development, and, when appropriate, assistance in dealing with personal or family concerns. It is possible for the officer to know his men, while still preserving the distinctions of rank which are essential to the effective operation of the organization. Knowledge of his men comes from daily observations of their work, how they function under stress, and how they respond to directions and work with others. This knowledge is essential in determining task assignments and strategy.

Enlisted Men

... mighty men of valor
Joshua I, 9

When the smoke cleared away it was the man with the sword, or the crossbow, or the rifle who settled the final issue on the field.
George Marshall to the NRA, 3 February 1939

Soldiers are the heart of a great army. The vast majority of any organization is composed of enlisted men. No matter how talented a commander or his officers may be, without the army they can achieve nothing. Unfortunately, very few people see the value in entry-level work, which requires long hours, tedious duties, and very few material rewards. But the entry-level position teaches the first lessons of skill and leadership. Few people have the luxury—or the misfortune—to start at the top. Those who do rarely have the discipline or the experience to succeed. A soldier beginning his career should see it as just that—a beginning. The history of both battle and business demonstrates that some of the greatest leaders had the most humble beginnings. Just as there are distinctions within the officer corp, the enlisted ranks are divided between noncommissioned officers and soldiers.

NONCOMMISSIONED OFFICERS
(Foreman, Shift or Team Leader)

The choice of noncommissioned officers is an object of the greatest importance: the order and discipline of a regiment depends so much upon their behavior that too much care cannot be taken in preferring none to that trust but those who by their merit and good conduct are entitled to it. Honesty, sobriety, and a remarkable attention to every point of duty, with a neatness in their dress, are indispensable requisites, nor can a sergeant or corporal be said to be qualified who does not write and read in a tolerable manner.

Baron von Steuben, Regulations for Order and Discipline of the Troops of the U.S., 1779

Any officer can get by on his sergeants. To be a sergeant you have to know your stuff. I'd rather be an outstanding sergeant than just another officer.

Sgt. Dan Daly, USMC, Winner of two Congressional Medals of Honor, 1873–1937

SOLDIER
(Entry-Level Employee)

Readiness, obedience and a sense of humor are the virtues of a soldier.

Brasidas of Sparta, Speech before battle of Amphipolis, 422 B.C.

What are the qualities of the good soldier by the development of which we make a man worthy—fit for any war? . . . The following four in whatever order you place them pretty well cover the field: discipline, physical fitness, technical skill in the use of his weapons, battlecraft.

Sir A. P. Wavell, 15 February 1933

Just as there are three general principles that characterize officers, there are three principles that should be mastered by the soldier: pride in his work, his unit, and himself.

PRIDE IN HIS WORK

When given a task, the soldier does it correctly and promptly. Whether marching across the parade ground or tooling a piece of machinery, every movement is precise. He takes pride in his work, whether or not his movements are being watched by superiors or colleagues. Personal pride dictates quality control.

PRIDE IN HIS UNIT

Just as the soldier takes pride in his work, it is important that he help create a sense of pride within the team. Collective pride in a job well done is a powerful force that will create bonds between fellow soldiers that last long past the completion of the current task at hand. Furthermore, this sense of unit pride helps sustain and motivate all to give their best. In combat, the soldier must rely on others. He will be far more willing to put himself at risk to protect the unit if he can depend upon others to do the same for him.

PRIDE IN HIMSELF

The soldier should make a daily effort in his dress, attitude, and conduct. He should ask himself, "Do I look, think, and act like a soldier?" If needed, he must then identify the areas that require improvement and make changes promptly. If he already measures up in all areas, he should consider whether he is taking the necessary steps for advancement. Greater rewards and responsibility come to those who seek them. Promotions are given not merely for past performance but also in expectation of future effort.

Discipline, Training, and Morale

B attle is a contest of wills, and the collective will of any organization is a factor of three broad and interrelated elements; namely, discipline, training, and morale. Each has a direct impact upon the others and is itself a product of many factors. In this section, we will address their key elements.

Discipline

Without discipline . . . a military corps or a ship's crew are no better than a disorderly mob; it is well-formed discipline that gives force, preserves order, obedience, and cleanliness, and causes alertness and dispatch in the execution of business.

Admiral Richard Kempenfeldt, RN, 28 December 1779

To ensure the successful operation of an army, corporation, or team, there must be a set of rules that govern the organization's day-to-day conduct. In recent years the concept of discipline has been criticized as either too stifling of creativity or destructive to the individual's sense of self-esteem. Yet it is unfair to equate discipline with mere stupidity. It is likewise inaccurate to view discipline as an end, as opposed to a means by which an end is achieved.

The methods for maintaining discipline have varied over time but generally fall into two schools: those who rely on fear and punishment and those who use positive persuasion to produce results. Whatever the method, those in charge must maintain a proper perspective and a sense of fairness.

The quotations that follow not only offer a persuasive argument for maintaining discipline but also reveal the varying methods by which discipline is to be achieved and maintained.

When every man is his own master in battle, he will readily find a decent excuse for saving himself.

Brasides of Sparta, Speech to Lacademonian Army, 423 B.C.

No state can be either happy or secure that is remiss and negligent in the discipline of its troops.

Vegetius, De Re Militari, 378 B.C.

The strength of an army lies in strict discipline and undeviating obedience to orders.

Thucydides, The History of the Peloponnesian Wars, 404 B.C.

Discipline is the soul of an army. It makes small numbers formidable; procures success to the weak and esteem to all.

George Washington to the Captains of the Virginia Regiment, 29 July 1759

It was an inflexible maxim of the Roman discipline that a good soldier should dread his own officers far more than the enemy.

Edward Gibbons, The Decline and Fall of the Roman Empire, 1776

Popularity; however desirable it may be to individuals, will not form or feed or pay an army; will not enable it to march, and fight; will not keep it in a state of efficiency for long and arduous service.

Wellington, Letter, 8 April 1811

As the severity of military operations increases, so also must the sternness of the discipline . . . when fortune is dubious or adverse; when retreats as well as advances are necessary, when supplies fail, arrangements miscarry, and disasters impend, and when the struggle is protracted, men can only be persuaded to accept evil things by the lively realization of the fact that greater terror awaits their refusal.

Winston Churchill, The River War, 1899

I don't mind being called tough, since I find in this racket it's the tough guys who lead the survivors.

Col. (later Gen.) Curtis Le May, 1943

There is only one sort of discipline—perfect discipline. If you do not enforce and maintain discipline, you are potential murders.

George S. Patton, Instructions to Third Army Commanders, 1944

Be swift to hear, slow to speak, slow to wrath.

James 1:19

There are two systems which generally speaking, divide the disciplinarians, the one is that of training men like spaniels by the stick; the other . . . substituting the point of honor in place of severity. The followers of the first are for reducing the nature of man as low as it will bear. The admirers of the latter are for exalting rationality, and they are commonly deceived in their expectations. . . . I apprehend a just medium between the two extremes to be the best means to bring English soldiers to perfection.

Major General John Burgoyne, Code of Instruction for 15th Dragoons, 1762

Willing obedience always beat forced obedience.

Xenophon, Cyropaedia, 430–350 B.C.

If troops are punished before their loyalty is secured they will be disobedient . . . Thus, command them with civility and imbue them uniformly with martial ardor and it may be said victory is certain . . . When orders are consistently trustworthy and observed, the relationship of the commander with his troops is satisfactory.

Sun Tzu, The Art of War, 400–320 B.C.

The superior man is firm in the right way, and not merely firm.

Confucius, Analects, 551–478 B.C.

When one treats people with benevolence, justice and righteousness and reposes confidence in them, the army will be united in mind and all will be happy to serve their leaders.

Chang Y, A.D. 1000

One can be exact and just, and beloved at the same time as feared. Severity must be accompanied by kindness, but this should not have the appearance of pretense, but of goodness.

Maurice de Saxe, Mes Rêveries, 1832

The discipline that makes the soldiers of a free country reliable in battle is not to be gained by harsh and tyrannical treatment. On the contrary, such treatment is far more likely to destroy than make an army. It is possible to give commands in such a manner and in such a tone of voice as to inspire in the soldier no feeling but the intense desire to obey, while the opposite manner and tone of voice

cannot fail to excite strong resentment and a desire to dis-
obey.

Major Gen. J. M. Schofield to the cadets at West Point, 1831–1906

How do we instill discipline? In addition to enforcing formal rules, there are several tools that help create
discipline within an organization.

SENSE OF DUTY

Every soldier deserves to know what is expected of
him, and leaders should do everything possible to cultivate a sense of duty in their men. The standards of performance should be clear. When the individual meets
the standards, he should merit the pay and privileges of
someone who has done his job. If he exceeds the stan-
dard, he should be rewarded, and if he fails to meet expectations, he should be disciplined. Rewarding an
individual for doing what is expected (i.e., showing up on
time, accomplishing a routine task) does nothing to
make him a better soldier because it creates a false impression of success. It also cheapens the work of those
who meet the standards out of a sense of duty.

In doing what we ought, we deserve no praise, because it
is our duty.

St. Augustine, A.D. 354–430

UNIFORMS

A uniform helps create the image of an army. The job of the military leader involves ensuring that uniforms are properly worn and convey an image of power and consistency. In many major corporations, dress guidelines exist and every member of the organization should follow them. Appropriate customs and courtesies are also important because they help foster an internal attitude of discipline and corporate identity. Proper decorum and dress convey strength and confidence to clients as well as competitors.

> A well-dressed soldier has more respect for himself. He also appears more redoubtable to the enemy and dominates him; for a good appearance is itself a force.
> Joseph Joubert, 1759–1824

> If you can't get them to salute when they should salute and wear the clothes you tell them to wear, how are you going to get them to die for their country?
> George S. Patton, 1885–1945

EVALUATIONS

Systematic evaluation of individual performance is essential to maintaining discipline and creating a winning army. Evaluations, both informal (at the end of the day) and formal (at scheduled periods), provide the individual with a means to assess his value to the team. A leader responsible for the supervision of others should maintain a notebook with an entry for every man. When the time for formal evaluations arrives, this notebook will prove invaluable in presenting a clear picture of the individual's total performance. Entries serve to justify promotions and rewards, as well as document poor performance. If the individual rates real praise, give it. If he doesn't, say so. The supervisor has to be man enough to state his true opinion if he expects the individual to benefit from it.

Personally I would not breed from this officer.
Remark on a cavalry officer's efficiency report, 1900

This officer has the manners of an organ-grinder and the morals of his monkey. I am unable to report on his work, as he has done none. . . .
Excerpt from a British Army fitness report

Training

To lead an untrained people to war is to throw them away.
Confucius, Analacts, xiii, 500 B.C.

An army raised without proper regard to the choice of its recruits was never made good by length of time.
Vegetius, De Re Militari, 378 B.C.

So sensible were the Romans of the imperfection of valor without skill and practice that, in their language, the name of an Army was borrowed from the word which signified exercise.
Edward Gibbon, The Decline and Fall of the Roman Empire, 1776

T raining is essential to the success of the unit. Yet the quality of the people chosen to be trained is as important as the quality of training that they are to be given. When selecting a recruit for a position at any level, the supervisor must consider both the individual's ability and his potential to assume greater responsibility. Standards should never be compromised. In time, the new recruit will make decisions that affect not only the army but other people's lives as well.

The greater problem faced today is the need to fill non-supervisory positions when there are more positions than qualified applicants. While an army or a company's mission is neither primary education nor social work, they may have to enter this field if personnel shortages are having an adverse effect on mission performance. In these circumstances, the organization and the prospective recruit must be prepared to make extra efforts.

Once the army has been assembled, continuous training is necessary. Those doing the training should be among the best the army or company has to offer. After all, training is an investment in the future. All too often, however, the amount of time and resources committed to training is sacrificed as the demands for budget cuts or short-term operational needs increase. While this trade-off might make sense for the short term, the long-term result is a weaker force that has not kept pace with advancements.

> For they had learned that true safety was to be found in long previous training and not in eloquent exhortations uttered when they were going into action.
>
> Thucydides, The History of the Peloponnesian Wars, 404 B.C.

> These men as soon as enlisted, should be taught to work on entrenchments, to march in ranks, to carry heavy burdens, and bear the sun and dust. Their meals should be coarse and moderate; they should be accustomed to lie sometimes in the open air and sometimes in tents. After this they should be instructed in the use of their arms. And if any long expedition is planned, they should be encamped as far as possible from the temptations of the city.
>
> Vegetius, De Re Militari, 378 B.C.

A government is the murderer of its citizens which sends them to the field uninformed and untaught, where they are to meet men of the same age and strength, mechanized by education and discipline for battle.

Harry "Light Horse" Lee, 1756–1818

Untutored courage is useless in the face of educated bullets.

George S. Patton, Cavalry Journal, 1922

Train in difficult, trackless, wooded terrain. War makes extremely heavy demands on the soldier's strength and nerves. For this reason, make heavy demands on your men in peacetime.

Erwin Rommel, Infantry Attacks, 1937

Morale

The Pentagon Whiz Kids are, I think, conscientious, patriotic people who are experts at calculating odds, figuring cost-effectiveness and squeezing the last cent out of contract negotiations. But they are heavy-handed butchers in dealing with that delicate, vital thing called "morale." This is the stuff that makes ships like the <u>Enterprise</u>, puts flags on Iwo Jima and wins wars. But I doubt if Mr. McNamara and his crew have a morale setting on their computers.

Adm. Daniel Gallery, <u>Eight Bells and All Is Well</u>, 1965

Creating a positive sense of morale is one of the most important and difficult tasks a commander faces. Little can be accomplished without a positive attitude. And sustaining morale requires daily maintenance. A commander's first task is to get an accurate picture of the state of morale of his unit. What is the appearance of the work area and the men of the unit? What is the level of disciplinary problems, absenteeism, and turnover? How well do the men perform their basic jobs? What is the attitude of the unit's leaders toward their job and one another? After taking these factors into account, the commander has to act, addressing what appears to be the most pressing concern and its causes. Discipline and training have a direct impact on morale, but there are several other contributive factors, and these are considered on the following pages.

By no means does the outcome of the battle depend upon numbers, but upon the united hearts of those who fight.

Kusnoki Masushige, Fourteenth century A.D.

A battle is lost less through the loss of men than by discouragement.

Frederick the Great, Instructions to His Generals, 1747

No system of tactics can lead to victory when the morale of an army is bad.

Jomini, Précis sur l'art de la Guerre, 1838

Morale is a state of mind. It is steadfastness and courage and hope . . . It is staying power, the spirit which endures to the end—the will to win. With it all things are possible, without it everything else, planning, preparation, production, count for naught.

Gen. George C. Marshall, Trinity College, 14 June 1941

Machines are as nothing without men. Men are as nothing without morale.

Adm. E. J. King to the graduates of Annapolis, 19 June 1942

If the history of military organization proves anything, it is that those units that are told that they are second-class will almost inevitably prove that they are second-class.

Brig. Gen. J. D. Hittle, USMC, The National Guardsman, July 1962

PAY

If an organization hopes to retain quality people it has to offer them a living wage and the prospect for advancement. People may first be drawn to the Army or company for reasons other than money—adventure, the opportunity to learn skills—but if a man has no hope of supporting himself and his family or if his talent is not valued, economic realities will lead him elsewhere. When he goes he takes his experience with him.

> Great things cannot be bought for small sums.
> Seneca, 4 B.C.–A.D. 65

> Without going into detail about the different rates of pay, I shall only say that it should be ample . . . Economy can only be pushed to a certain point. It has limits beyond which it degenerates into parsimony.
> Maurice de Saxe, Mes Rêveries, 1732

> There must be some other stimulus besides love for the country, to make men fond of service.
> George Washington, 1732–99

ESPRIT DE CORPS

In building esprit de corps a leader seeks to establish a group identity and pride for the organization through shared efforts, sacrifice, and success. A leader needs to foster this team spirit, because, although an organization is made up of individuals, in order to be effective, these individuals must be directed to a common goal. And, in the crush of battle, a warrior will risk death or die for the small group if men with whom he has shared goals and experience. Esprit de corps can be fostered most effectively in the after-duty hours either through sport, shared meals, or social gatherings. These events shouldn't place undue demands on the man's after-hours time but should be seen as informal and voluntary opportunities for establishing camaraderie and friendship.

We few, we happy few, we band of brothers . . .

Shakespeare, Henry V, iv

All that can be done with the soldier is to give him esprit de corps—i.e., a higher opinion of his own regiment than all other troops of his country.

Frederick the Great, Military Testament, 1768

I have eaten your bread and salt. I have drunk
your water and wine. The deaths ye died I
have watched beside, And the lives you led were mine.
Was there aught that I did not share
In vigil, toil or ease—One joy or woe that I did not
know Dear hearts across the seas?

Rudyard Kipling, Departmental Ditties, 1885

Esprit de Corps thrives not only on success, but on hardships and adversity shared with courage and fortitude.

Gen. Orlando Ward, USA, May 1965

You have got to see our forces as a human living organism and treat it as such.

Colin Powell, 1995

LOYALTY

Loyalty is a prime ingredient of high morale. Commanders should expect loyalty from every member of the unit. Opinions should be sought when needed, but once a decision is made, the commander has the right to expect that his orders will be carried out with dispatch. The commander inspires loyalty only if he demonstrates loyalty to his men. He must work tirelessly for the welfare of his unit, give credit where it is due, show no favoritism in his decisions, and accept responsibility for action taken on his watch.

> Grant stood by me when I was crazy, and I stood by him when he was drunk, and now we stand by each other.
>
> Attributed to W. T. Sherman, 1870

> There is a great deal of talk about loyalty from the bottom to the top. Loyalty from the top down is even more necessary and much less prevalent.
>
> George S. Patton, War As I Knew It, 1947

CIVIL WARS

Rivalry within an organization is a double-edged sword. An environment of fierce competition forces each division to strive to be the best. But when healthy rivalry gives way to resentment or contempt, the commander must act quickly to prevent personal animosity from jeopardizing the mission. Likewise, rumors and gossip can undermine unit cohesion. Commanders can avoid these pitfalls by keeping their men involved and informed.

> There is nothing unhappier than a civil war, for the conquered are destroyed by and the conquerors destroy their friends.
>
> Dionysius of Halicarnassus, Antiquities of Rome, 20 B.C.

> In a calamity any rumor is believed.
>
> Publilus Syrus, Sententiae, #17, 50 B.C.

> Such men as he be never at heart's ease
> Whiles they behold a greater than themselves,
> And therefore are they very dangerous.
>
> Shakespeare, Julius Caesar, I, ii

> Contempt is a kind of gangrene, which if it seizes on part of a character, corrupts the rest.
>
> Samuel Johnson, Works, vol. iii, 1709–84

Every man hath in his own life sins enough, in his own mind trouble enough, in his own fortune evil enough, and in the performance of his office more than enough to entertain his own inquiries . . .

Jeremy Taylor, Holy Living, 1613–67

AWARDS

While high standards are to be expected of every man, it is appropriate from time to time to recognize truly superior performance. But rewards should be doled out judiciously. If awards are given too freely, their value is diminished. If they are given unwisely, they create resentment.

To those young men who, either in war or other circumstances, have deserved commendation, prizes should be given.

Plato, 428–317 B.C.

Show me a republic, ancient or modern, in which there have been no decorations. Some people call them baubles. Well, it is by such baubles that one leads men.

Napoleon I, Remarks on establishing the Legion of Honor, 19 May 1802

REPRIMANDS

Occasionally a commander must reprimand a member of his unit. Reprimands, to be effective, should be concise and delivered in private. The commander's goal is to correct errors or faulty performance—not public humiliation. When appropriate, the mistake should be made clear, the proper course of action identified, and a directive given for future conduct. The person in error is far more likely to respond without resentment if he has not been humiliated before his colleagues.

Admonish your friends in private. Praise them in public.
Publilus Syrus, Sententiae, 50 B.C.

Never give a man a dollar's worth of blame without a dime's worth of praise.
Col. L. P. Hunt, USMC, 1937

PART III

PREPARING

FOR BATTLE

Preparation for and the conduct of battle is a complex endeavor. To be successful it must be the product of detailed planning and an effective division of labor. This is true for the largest unit as well as the two-man operation. Staffs of large units are divided into four principal sections: the 1 (Administration), the 2 (Intelligence), the 3 (Operations and Plans), and the 4 (Logistics and Maintenance). The primary reason for this division of tasks is that one man is unable to perform all the functions needed to support a large organization. While the commander retains overall responsibility for the accomplishment of each function, he delegates authority to his principal staff officers to accomplish specific tasks. Each section is concerned with its own function, but it must work in tandem with the others.

Administration

(Human Resources)

A certain amount of administrative work is necessary in any organization. People have to be paid, records kept, correspondence answered. The danger is to confuse administration, which facilitates the accomplishment of the mission, with the mission itself. No enemy soldier was ever killed by a memo. Commanders must keep administrative demands to a bare minimum and constantly guard against making their soldiers slaves to administrative burdens.

Do the business of the day in the day.

Wellington, Letter from Portugal, 1811

My Lord,
If I attempted to answer the mass of futile correspondence
that surrounds me, I should be debarred from all serious
business of campaigning . . . I shall see that no officer
under my Command is debarred, by attending to the futile drivelling of mere quill driving in your Lordship's office from attending to his first duty—which is, and always
has been, so to train the private men under his command
that they may, without question, beat any force opposed
to them in the field.

Attributed to Wellington from a British training circular, 1941

Paper-work will ruin any military force.

Lewis "Chesty" Puller, Marine, 1962

Administration is something to be got on with not deified.

Michael Ramsey, Interview, 1962

Communications and Correspondence

There is a tendency to confuse the length of a correspondence with its importance. The most essential information can often be communicated in the fewest words. Reports or orders should be accurate, clear, timely, and concise. Brevity is not only the soul of wit, it is a critical aspect of an efficient exchange of information.

I came, I saw, I conquered.

Julius Caesar, Dispatch to the Roman Senate after the Battle of Zela, 47 B.C.

I am your King. You are a Frenchman.
There is the enemy. Charge!

Henry IV of France, Battle of Iury, 14 March 1590

Scratch one flat-top.

Cmdr. Robert Dixon, USN, Battle of the Coral Sea, Report of sinking the Japanese carrier <u>Shoho</u>, 7 May 1942

Sighted sub, sank same.

Lt. Donald F. Mason, USN, 8 January 1942

Section 2

Intelligence

(Know the Competition, Market Research,
Concealing Your Corporate Strategy from
Competitors)

J ust as it is crucial to know the strengths and weaknesses of your own ranks, it is essential to know as
much as possible about the enemy forces. Decisions
made in a vacuum are often wrong. Military commanders
and corporate decision makers rarely have exact knowledge of their enemies' plans before they act. But crucial
information can be gleaned from "open sources" which
include speeches, annual reports, surveys, new weapons

or product displays. Successful military commanders learn that all information is valuable. Remember, knowledge is power and what may at first seem insignificant may have great importance.

> Agitate the enemy and ascertain the pattern of his movements. Determine his dispositions and so ascertain the fields of battle. Probe him and learn where his strength is abundant and where deficient.
>
> Sun Tzu, The Art of War, 400–320 B.C.

> The art of war is divided between force and stratagem. What cannot be accomplished by force must be done by stratagem.
>
> Frederick the Great, Instruction to His Generals, xii, 1747

> When I took a decision or adopted an alternative it was after studying every relevant—and many irrelevant factors. Geography, tribal structure, religion, social customs, language, appetites, standards—all were at my finger-ends. The enemy I knew almost like my own side. I risked myself among them a hundred times to learn.
>
> T. E. Lawrence (Lawrence of Arabia), 1933

> To achieve victory we must as far as possible make the enemy blind and deaf by sealing his eyes and ears, and drive his commanders to distraction by creating confusion in their minds.
>
> Mao Tse-tung, On Protracted War, 1893–1976

Operations

The Operations staff is concerned with the operational functions of the command, its contacts with supporting units or allies (in corporate terms, distributors and sales representatives) and the enemy (the competition) on the battlefield. Specifically, the mission of "the 3" involves: **Preparedness**—readying the command for any type of battle; **Strategy**—the development of overall goals and the concrete means to achieve them; **Plans**—the specific details by which the operation will be undertaken based on a continuous estimate of the situation; and **Tactics**—the methods to be employed in battle with consideration of the factors of time and surprise. Following is a discussion of each of these functions.

Preparedness

(Maintaining Corporate Health, Market Value, and a Competitive Edge)

Preparedness—achieving the state of readiness necessary for combat in terms of men, material, and training—is a task best accomplished before war begins. It is difficult enough to achieve under the best of conditions, and it may be impossible to do so once under heavy attack. The Operations staff, in conjunction with the other staff officers, must continuously and realistically assess the unit and act decisively to correct shortcomings. This analysis encompasses every aspect of the command's functions: the status of personnel, training equipment, and supplies. In addition, to maintain the competitive edge of the unit as a whole, the operations section, with help from the intelligence staff, needs to continuously evaluate the abilities of prospective opponents.

> It is a doctrine of war not to assume the enemy will not come, but rather to rely on one's readiness to meet him; not to presume that he will not attack, but rather to make one's self invincible.
>
> Sun Tzu, The Art of War, 400–320 B.C.

> Chariots strong, horses fast, troops valiant, weapons sharp—so that when they hear the drums beat the attack

they are happy, and when they hear the gongs sound the retirement they are enraged. He who is like this is strong.

Chang Yu, 1000

A wise man in time of peace prepares for war.

Horace, Satires II, c. 30 B.C.

The man who is prepared has his battle half fought.

Cervantes, Don Quixote, 1605

The country must have a large and efficient army, one capable of meeting the enemy abroad, or they must expect to meet him at home.

Wellington, Letter, 28 January 1811

Strategy and Objectives

(Formulating the Big Picture and Long-Term Plan)

Strategy is the clearly defined goal to which all action is directed. The strategic plan consists of a series of concrete objectives, the achievement of which constitutes victory. In World War II, for example, the strategic plan was the defeat of the Axis powers, first in Europe, then in Asia. A series of objectives was outlined for battle in each theater. Although this contest involved the participation of literally millions of people across the globe, the strategic goal was present in everyone's mind.

Once the strategy is defined, a series of objectives are determined by which the goal will be achieved. The objectives must be broad enough not only to encompass the intermediate goals but also to look to the future once the object is obtained. When a commander gives a platoon leader a simple order such as "Take the hill," the platoon leader only knows he is to attack the hill and seize it. The order doesn't say what he is to do when he gets to the top. Should he continue the attack if conditions are favorable? How much should he risk to achieve the goal? The stated objective must look past the intermediate steps to the final goal of the big picture.

Where there is no vision the people perish.
Proverbs 29:18

If a man does not know to what port he is steering, no wind is favorable.

Seneca, 4 B.C.–65 A.D.

It is no doubt a good thing to conquer on the field of battle, but it needs greater wisdom and greater skill to make use of victory.

Polybius, Histories, 125 B.C.

There is occasions and causes why and wherefore in all things.

Shakespeare, Henry V, Act V

Pursue one great decisive aim with force and determination.

Clausewitz, Principles of War, 1812

Plans

Plans are the directions to be followed in a battle or campaign. These directions should be as simple as possible and clearly communicated. They also must correspond to the realities confronting the commander who is supervising their implementation. And finally, they should allow for some flexibility. Ideally, a plan is the product of thorough and thoughtful preparation. It not only directs the desired action but also tries to anticipate an enemy's response. Planners must also weigh the time needed for preparation against current circumstances. In some cases the speed of response is more critical than ensuring that every possible outcome is considered. In these instances planners must ascertain that their directions at the very least address the who, what, where, when, and why of each situation so that opportunity and action are maximized.

> A good plan violently executed NOW is better than a perfect plan next week.
> George S. Patton, War As I Knew It, 1947

> With many calculations, one can win; with few one cannot. How much less chance of victory has one who makes none at all! By this means I examine the situation and the outcome will be clearly apparent.
> Sun Tzu, The Art of War, 400–320 B.C.

A general is not easily overcome who can form a true judgment of his own and the enemy's forces.

Vegetius, <u>De Re Militari</u>, 378 B.C.

The ability of a commander to comprehend a situation and act promptly is the talent which great men have of conceiving in a moment all the advantages of the terrain and the use that they can make of it with their army.

Frederick the Great, Instructions for His Generals, 1747

An educated guess is just as accurate and far faster than compiled errors.

George S. Patton, <u>War As I Knew It</u>, 1947

Be audacious and cunning in your plans, firm and persevering in their execution, determined to find a glorious end.

Clausewitz, <u>Principles of War</u>, 1812

The stroke of genius that turns the fate of battle? I don't believe it. A battle is a complicated operation, that you prepare laboriously. If the enemy does this, you say to yourself, I will do that . . . You think out every possible development and decide how to deal with the situation created. One of these developments occurs, you put your plan in operation, and everyone says "What genius . . ." whereas credit is really due to the labor of preparation.

Ferdinand Foch, Interview, 1919

Successful generals make plans to fit circumstances, but do not try to create circumstances to fit plans.

George S. Patton, <u>War As I Knew It</u>, 1947

Tactics

Tactics are the "how" of battle. They describe basic procedures for accomplishing a task. Whether taking a hill, creating a product, or closing a sale, certain fundamentals are observed in any profession. The commander must ensure that all hands master the fundamentals, while still maintaining an awareness of changes in technology, weapons, or enemy capabilities. A wise tactician seeks to fully utilize the strengths of his unit and exploit the weakness of his competitor. On the battlefield, the general seeks to avoid attacking an enemy's fixed position (the point of his greatest strength) by attacking him from the flank or rear. Similar tactics should be employed on the corporate battlefield. If the competitor's strength is price or distribution, undercut him with quality or service. If quality is comparable, attack through speed, applications, or innovations.

It is an invariable axiom of war to secure your own flanks and rear and endeavor to turn those of your enemy.
Frederick the Great, Instructions for His Generals, 1747

It is an accepted maxim of war, never to do what the enemy wishes you to do, for this reason alone, that he desires it; avoid a battlefield he has reconnoitered and studied, and with even more reason, ground that he has fortified and where he is entrenched.
Napoleon I, Maxims of War, 1831

There is only one tactical principle which is not subject to change. It is: to use the means at hand to inflict the maximum amount of wounds, death and destruction on the enemy in the minimum of time.

George S. Patton, <u>War As I Knew It</u>, 1947

TIME AND OPPORTUNITY

Time is a tactical resource. Everyone receives the exact same allocation every day, and whoever makes the best use of time enjoys an advantage in combat. Commanders must guard against wasting not only their own time but also that of their subordinates. Endless meetings, excessive administrative burdens, and poor scheduling are thieves; treat them as such.

Opportunities that present themselves on the battlefield are a product of the quality of the commander's tactical planning, the mistakes of the enemy, or chance. The ability to recognize opportunities is a factor of both experience and intuition. When they present themselves they must not be squandered.

Four things come not back:
The spoken word; the sped arrow;
Time past; the neglected opportunity.

Omar Ibn, <u>Sayings</u>, 541–644

Time is everything; five minutes makes the difference between victory and defeat.

Lord Nelson, 1758–1805

. . . too late? Ah! two fatal words of this war! Too late in moving here. Too late in arriving there. Too late in coming to this decision. Too late in starting with enterprises. Too late in preparing. In this war the footsteps of the Allied Forces have been dogged by the mocking specter of "Too Late"!

Lloyd George to the House of Commons, 20 December 1915

MAINTAINING THE OFFENSE

Victory is achieved through offensive tactics. Defensive operations only buy time to prepare for the resumption of the attack. The commander must keep this fact in mind. Continuous pursuit of the unit goal, whether it is the destruction of enemy forces or control of greater market share, must be the unfailing theme of all decisions.

The minds of men are apt to be swayed by what they hear; and they are most afraid of those who commence an attack.

Hermocrates of Syracuse, Speech to the Syracusians, 415 B.C.

The best thing for an army on the defensive is to know how to take the offensive at the proper time, and to take it.

Jomini, Précis sur l'art de la Guerre, 1836

For what is more thrilling than the sudden and swift development of an attack at dawn?

Winston Churchill, The River War, 1899

In war the only sure defense is offense, and the efficiency of the offense depends on the warlike souls of those conducting it.

George S. Patton, War As I Knew It, 1947

Mobility, Velocity, Indirect Approach!

Heinz Guderian, Definition of Blitzkrieg, 1950

SURPRISE

Surprise is a great tactic, but it is important that the action be well planned and well executed. History gives numerous examples of commanders who, having surprised the enemy, failed to accomplish their strategic aim. When contemplating a surprise attack the commander must ask himself two questions: What is the opportunity I seek to create? What will I do if I succeed in creating this opportunity?

The execution of a military surprise is always dangerous and the general who is never taken off his guard himself, and never loses an opportunity of striking at an unguarded foe, will be most likely to succeed in war.

Thucydides, The History of the Peloponnesian Wars, 404 B.C.

Always mystify, mislead and surprise the enemy if possible.

Stonewall Jackson, 1824–63

Logistics

(Supply and Maintenance)

L ogistics encompass a multitude of functions that are necessary to sustain an army. The supply and maintenance of men and equipment give the unit staying power in combat. These functions demand attention to detail and the ability to maximize resources, set priorities, and make decisions when logistical reality and plans do not coincide. No plan however daring or thoroughly conceived can succeed if the means and methods of execution are not regulated, maintained, and rehearsed.

Without supplies neither a general nor a soldier is good for anything.

Clearchus of Sparta, Speech to Greek Army in Asia Minor, 401 B.C.

For want of a nail, the shoe was lost—for want of a shoe, the horse was lost—for want of a horse, the rider was lost—for want of a rider, the battle was lost.

George Herbert, Outlandish Proverbs, 1640

Logistics comprises the means and arrangements which work out the plans of strategy and tactics. Strategy decides where to act; logistics brings the troops to this point.

Jomini, Précis sur l'art de la Guerre, 1838

Seeing what had been thrown away I wondered how the battle had been fought.

Remark by a Union officer after Cold Harbor, June 1864

The cards in the game of life are the characters of men. . . . But when we play the game of death, things are our counters—guns, rivers, shells, bread, roads, forests, ships.

Sir Ian Hamilton, Gallipoli Diary, 1920

The onus of supply rests equally on the giver and the taker.

George S. Patton, War As I Knew It, 1947

PART IV

COROLLARIES
AND CAUTIONS

The following quotations are offered as points for leaders to consider as they prepare for and wage battle. In the first three sections of this book we have examined the positive aspects of military leadership and organization. But it is important to remember that even the best of warriors—both military and corporate—must contend with human foibles and fears in their men and in themselves.

Dealing with a
Defeated Enemy

. . . for when lenity and cruelty play for a kingdom, the gentler gamester is the soonest winner.

Shakespeare, <u>Henry V</u>, III, vi

Decisiveness

I object to having to say things twice.

Plautus, <u>Pseudolus</u>, 254–184 B.C.

Difficulties

Everything is simple in war, but the simplest thing is difficult. These difficulties accumulate and produce a friction which no man can imagine exactly who has not seen war.

Clausewitz, On War, 1832

Fear

Fear makes men forget, and skill which cannot fight is useless.

Phormio of Athens, Before action in the Crisaen Gulf, 429 B.C.

Fear makes men ready to believe the worst.

Quintus Curtius Rufus, De Rebus Gesti Alexandri Magni, A.D. 200

Indecision

What can be more detestable than to be continually changing our minds?

Cleon of Athens, Speech to the Athenians, 427 B.C.

An irresolute general, acting without rule or plan, although at the head of an army superior in number to that of the enemy, finds himself almost always inferior on the field of battle.

Napoleon I, Maxims, 1831

Keeping an Open Mind

Victory smiles upon those who anticipate the changes in the character of war, not upon those who wait to adapt themselves after they occur.

Giulo Douhet, <u>Command of the Air</u>, 1921

The only thing harder than getting a new idea into the military mind is to get an old one out.

Liddell Hart, <u>Thoughts on War</u>, 1944

Prejudice against innovation is a typical characteristic of an officer corps which has grown up in a well-tried and proven system.

Erwin Rommel, <u>The Rommel Papers</u>, 1953

Leading by Committee

If a man consults whether to fight when he has the power in his own hands, it is certain that his opinion is against fighting.

Nelson, Letter to Viscount Sidmouth, August 1801

A council of war never fights, and in a crisis the duty of the leader is to lead and not take refuge in the generally timid wisdom of a multitude of councilors.

Theodore Roosevelt, Autobiography, 1913

A conference of subordinates to collect ideas is the resort of a weak commander.

Montgomery of Alamein, Memoirs, 1958

Learn from Your Enemies

It is right to learn, even from the enemy.

Ovid, Metamorphoses, A.D. 8

Micromanagement

If therefore, anyone thinks himself qualified to give advice respecting the war I am to conduct, let him come with me to Macedonia . . . but if he thinks this too much trouble, and prefers the repose of the city life to the toils of war, let him not on the land, assume to the office of the pilot.

Lucius Amelius Paulus, Speech in Rome prior to departing for war, 168 B.C.

Never tell people how to do things. Tell them <u>what</u> to do and let them surprise you with their ingenuity.

George S. Patton, War As I Knew It, 1947

Orders

Remember, gentlemen, an order that can be misunderstood will be misunderstood.

Helmuth von Moltke, 1800–91

Overly Cautious Staffs

Experienced military men are familiar with the tendency that always has to be watched in staff work, to see all our own difficulties but to credit the enemy with the ability to do things we should not dream of attempting.

Sir John Slessor, Strategy for the West, 1954

Plans

Human beings, like plans, prove fallible in the presence of those things missing in maneuvers—danger, death, and live ammunition.

Barbara W. Tuchman, <u>The Guns of August</u>, 1962

Reputations

We cannot afford to confine the Army appointments to persons who have excited no hostile comment in their career . . . This is a time to try men of force and vision and not be exclusively confined to those judged thoroughly safe by conventional standards.

Winston Churchill, Note to the Imperial General Staff, 19 October 1940

Risk

The habit of gambling contrary to reasonable calculations
is a military vice which as the pages of history reveal, has
ruined more armies than any other cause.

Liddell Hart, Thoughts on War, 1944

Unforeseen Factors

In war we must always leave room for strokes of fortune,
and accidents that cannot be foreseen.

Polybius, Histories, 125 B.C.

You will usually find that the enemy has three courses
open to him, and of these he will adopt the fourth.

Helmuth von Moltke, 1800–91

Conclusion

Manfully
They stood, and everywhere with
gallant front Opposed in fair array the shock of
war. Desperately they fought, like men
expert in arms. And knowing that no safety could be
found Save from their own right hands.

Robert Southey, 1744–1843

I t is hoped that the preceding pages have offered some
insight into the soul of the warrior, leadership, and organization. The purpose of this book was not to ad-
vocate a new theory of management but to gather
wisdom from some of history's most able teachers. The
warriors, whose words and deeds have commanded these
pages, knew what it was to be tested under the most trying of circumstances. Though they fought in different

times and lands, they understood that while weapons and tactics may change, human nature remains constant. Today, we live in trying times and there is a sore need for heroes on many fronts—business, government, the military itself. If we are to rise to the challenges that face us, we have to rediscover the attributes and virtues that have always epitomized the warrior. The concepts of bravery, self-discipline, duty, and loyalty all require personal commitment and sacrifice, but their necessity on all of life's battlefields cannot be disputed. Those who choose to enter the fray can take comfort in this ancient adage:

The Hero's deeds and hard won fame shall live.

Ovid, <u>Lividum</u>, 43 B.C.–A.D. 18

Bibliography

Stephen E. Ambrose. *The Supreme Commander: The War Years of General Dwight D. Eisenhower* (New York: Doubleday, 1970).

Sir Gavin de Beer. *Hannibal: Challenging Rome's Supremacy* (New York: Viking, 1969).

Clay Blair. *The Forgotten War: America in Korea 1950–1953* (New York: Times Books, 1987).

Martin Bluemenson. *The Patton Papers: 1940–1945*, Vols. 1 and 2 (Boston: Houghton Mifflin, 1974).

Anthony Bridge. *The Crusades* (New York: Franklin Watts, 1982).

Carl von Clausewitz. *On War*, Edited and translated by Michael Howard and Peter Paret (Princeton: Princeton University Press, 1976).

———. *The Principles of War*, Edited and translated by Hans W. Gatzke. *Roots of Strategy*, Vol. 2 (Harrisburg: Stackpole, 1987).

Carlos D'Este. *Patton: A Genius for War* (New York: HarperCollins, 1995).

Dwight D. Eisenhower. *At Ease: Stories I Tell to Friends* (Garden City, N.Y.: Doubleday, 1967).

Bergen Evans. *Dictionary of Quotations* (New York: Dela-corte, 1968).

Ladislas Farago. *The Last Days of Patton* (New York: McGraw-Hill, 1981).

Hugo Baron von Freytag-Loringhoven. *The Power of Personality in War*, Translated by Historical Section, Army War College, *Roots of Strategy*, Vol. 3 (Harrisburg: Stackpole, 1991).

William K. Goolrick and Ogden Tanner, et al. *The Battle of the Bulge* (Alexandria, Va.: Time-Life, 1979).

Robert Debs Heinl, Jr. *The Dictionary of Military and Naval Quotations* (Annapolis, Md.: The U.S. Naval Institute Press, 1966).

Infantry Journal, Inc. *Infantry in Battle*, Marine Corps Association. 1939 ed. 2d reprint. 1986.

Rosemary Harvley Jarman. *Crispin Day: The Glory of Agincourt* (Boston: Little, Brown, 1979).

Antoine Henri Jomni. *The Art of War*, Edited by Brig. Gen. J. D. Hittle, *Roots of Strategy*, Vol. 2 (Harrisburg: Stackpole, 1987).

Douglas MacArthur. A *Soldier Speaks: Public Papers and Speeches of General of the Army Douglas MacArthur* (New York: Praeger, 1965).

Charles B. McDonald. A *Time for Trumpets: The Untold Story of the Battle of the Bulge* (New York: Morrow, 1985).

William Manchester. *American Caesar: Douglas MacArthur 1886–1964* (Boston: Little, Brown, 1978).

Allan R. Millet. *Semper Fidelis: The History of the United States Marine Corps* (New York: MacMillan, 1980).

William O'Connor-Morris. *Hannibal: Soldier, Statesman, Patriot* (New York: Putnam, 1897). Reprinted by AMS Press, 1987.

Leonard Mosley. *Marshall: Hero for Our Times* (New York: Hearst, 1982).

The New Jerusalem Bible (Garden City, N.Y.: Doubleday, 1985).

Sir Harris Nicholas. *The History of the Battle of Agincourt* (London: Barnes and Noble. Reprint by Redwood Press, 1970).

Morris E. Opler. *An Apache Lifeway* (New York: Cooper Square, 1965).

George S. Patton. *War As I Knew It* (Boston: Houghton Mifflin, 1947).

Brig. Gen. T. R. Philips, ed. *Roots of Strategy: The Five Greatest Military Classics of All Time* (Harrisburg: Stackpole, 1985).

Ardant du Picq. *Battle Studies*, Translated by Col. John N. Greeley and Maj. Robert C. Cotton, *Roots of Strategy*, Vol. 2 (Harrisburg: Stackpole, 1987).

Forrest C. Pogue. *George C. Marshall—Education of a General 1880–1939* (New York: Viking, 1963).

Colin Powell with Joseph E. Persico. *My American Journey* (New York: Random House, 1995).

Kate Louise Roberts, ed. *Hoyt's New Cyclopedia of Practical Quotations* (New York, Funk & Wagnalls 1958).

William Shakespeare. *The Complete Works* (Kingsport, Tenn.: Viking Press Ed., 1977).

Lisa Shaw, ed. *In His Own Words: Colin Powell* (New York: Perigee, 1995).

Brig. Gen. Edwin H. Simmons. *The United States Marines: The First Two Hundred Years 1775–1975* (New York: Viking, 1976).

Burton Stevens, ed. *The Home Book of Quotations*, 10th ed. (New York: 1967).

Robert A. Wilson, ed. *Character Above All* (New York: Simon & Schuster, 1995).

W. J. Wood. *Leaders and Battles: The Art of Military Leadership* (Novatica, Calif.: Presidio Press, 1984).

Desmond Young. *Rommel: The Desert Fox* (New York: Harper & Row, 1950).

ABOUT THE AUTHOR

Arthur L. Clark has a B.A. in history (Marquette) and a J.D. and an M.A. in international affairs (Catholic University). He graduated with distinction from the U.S. Naval War College and has served as research assistant in the Executive Office of the President. He is a Major in the United States Marine Corps Reserves, a certified Close Combat Instructor, and has held numerous Command and Staff positions while serving in the Marine Corps.